Floella Hits the Roof

Slowly, the dragon stretched his wings. Seb and Floella held their breath as the mended wing extended itself, then hung on for dear life as the dragon flapped both wings vigorously up and down.

"Might have waited for us to find a safe place," grumbled Floella.

Worse was to follow. Without a word of warning, the dragon, having found the wing in suitable condition, swivelled round and made a rapid vertical take-off, with Seb and Floella hanging on as best they could to the scales on its neck. As they gained height, the shouting, whirring and screaming from below was soon left behind.

JANE HOLIDAY

Floella Hits the Roof

Illustrated by Kate Simpson

For Amanda

This edition published 1994 by
Diamond Books
77–85 Fulham Palace Road
Hammersmith, London W6 8JB

First published in Young Lions 1989
Third impression April 1992

ISBN 0 261 66478 6

Printed and bound in Great Britain

1

A Surprise in Great Bootington

In Great Bootington it was a fine summer day. Many of the inhabitants were preparing, in different ways, for the visit of a very important person. Her Majesty the Queen was coming to the town for the official opening of the new maternity ward in Great Bootington Hospital.

The whole town was being refurbished for her visit. The streets were being specially cleaned and the buildings painted up. The railway station had been swept and redecorated and the Station Manager had a special red carpet ready for the great day. The Mayor of Great Bootington, Arthur Greenhalgh, was very excited. He bought a black suit to show off his gold chain better, as well as some new patent leather shoes. His wife Mavis decided on her outfit and her hairstyle. She even practised curtseying. She wasn't worried about meeting the Queen.

"She's just another woman," she said. "I reckon we'll get on grand." She *was* worried though about her son and daughter. Mike was unemployed and planned to join a demonstration at the railway station when the Queen arrived. Tracey had a job but didn't approve of the Royal Family at all.

"Kings and Queens are out of date," she said.

As usual when he had civic work to do, Arthur was picked up that fine Tuesday morning, in the Mayoral Ford Cortina. He said he'd feel silly in a Rolls and they used too much petrol anyway.

"Hey, what's that?" asked Arthur as they drove down Library Street. "Is there something going on?"

A crowd of people were standing outside the library and the D.H.S.S. Two or three people were standing in the middle of the road.

"Stop here, Bill," Arthur said to the chauffeur. "I want to see what's happening." He

walked briskly down the road. He was a bit too fat to run. A woman who worked in the town hall ran up to him:

"I said all along we shouldn't have a flat roof on the Town Hall, now didn't I?"

"Hey up, Maisie," said Arthur. "What are you on about? What's happened to the roof? Has it collapsed?"

He looked upwards. It looked much the same as usual to him, though he didn't know why so many people were hanging out of the windows. Over the road at the D.H.S.S., people were looking out of all the windows too.

"No, not yet," said Maisie, pushing a wisp of hair off her face. "Not *yet*. And just when we're getting ready for the Queen coming too."

"But . . . WHAT'S HAPPENED?" asked Arthur. "Why's everyone standing outside?"

He could see typists, secretaries, cleaners, the Chief Executive Officer, the Treasurer and the Accountant.

"There's a dragon on the roof," said one of the typists.

"You what?" said Arthur.

"It's true, Arthur," said one of the bystanders. It was the Housing Officer, Mr Singh. "Come with me. I'll show you."

Arthur followed him up the four flights of stairs of the Town Hall.

"Time to put in a lift," puffed Arthur.

"Allow me," said Mr Singh and helped him up the few remaining stairs. They stepped out onto a fairly wide balcony from which an iron ladder ran up to the roof.

"No further," said Arthur.

"No indeed," said Mr Singh. "It would be most unsafe. Look."

Arthur looked.

"Gracious heaven," he exclaimed. "It *is* a dragon."

The dragon was a big one, well over eighteen metres long. It was an emerald green colour with scales tipped in gold. It had a golden tail forked at the end. Long golden claws glittered on its feet. The head was huge with golden jaws and a purple face with blood red eyes. From where the two men stood, they could see only its profile. A neat purple wing stretched from its body. The dragon turned its head slightly towards them. Smoke belched from its jaws.

9

Arthur and Mr Singh retreated.

By the time they reached the ground floor, everyone had disappeared back to work and the police had cordoned off Library Street and Court Street with traffic cones.

Arthur and the Chief Executive Officer discussed what should be done over a cup of tea and a Rich Tea biscuit.

"It was one of the typists spotted it first," said Mr Gorse. "She heard a terrible thump – said it shook the building – and went out to see what had happened. Had to send her home it was such a shock."

"Aye, it must be a fair weight. No wonder Maisie was talking about the roof collapsing. So what are we going to do about it, Malachi?"

"I've got the police on to it. We'll see what they come up with first," Mr Gorse said. "But we haven't much time, what with the Queen due on Thursday."

"Aye," said Arthur. "Still, the police should know what to do."

At that moment Police Constable Barrow was reporting back to his sergeant.

"So what was it then, Barrow? Has everyone in Great Bootington gone completely bonkers? What was on the roof of the Town Hall? A flying saucer? An unexploded bomb? Or just a piece of rubbish fallen out of a plane?"

PC Barrow cleared his throat.

"Well Barrow? I'm waiting lad."

"Please sir," said Barrow, going as red as a pillar-box, "it was a dragon."

Sergeant Fraser's eyebrows rose two inches.

"Really?" he said. "So . . . what did you do, then?"

"Well sir, I got hold of a traffic warden and she served it with a parking ticket and . . ."

"*You blanketty what?*" bellowed Sergeant Fraser.

PC Barrow looked sullen.

"They don't teach us owt about dragons at police college . . . sir."

"Served it with a parking ticket. I don't think they teach you anything nowadays," said Sergeant Fraser, shaking his head in disbelief.

"What would you have done, sir?"

Sergeant Fraser reached for his pipe and that gave him inspiration.

11

"Not our job Barrow," he said. "It's a fire hazard, that's what it is. Give the fire brigade a bell."

"Right sir."

The fire brigade decided it wasn't their job either. One fireman had fallen off a ladder and been taken off to Great Bootington Infirmary, two more were overcome by fumes which the dragon emitted when they attempted to hose him down, three more firemen were swept off by the fierce lashing of its tail and were caught in a safety net held up after the accident to the first man.

After this the Chief Fireman called all his men off. When the hose had been rewound onto the wagon and his men (those who were left) assembled, he made a statement.

"We are reporting back to our Union," he said. "It is not laid down anywhere in our conditions of service that we have to extinguish fire-breathing . . . creatures. We have three men detained in hospital indefinitely and three more suffering from shock will be released, I understand, this evening. Come on, men."

The firemen leapt back onto their wagon

and took off at full tilt down the bottom of Library Street. Frantic phone calls were made to different firms with cranes. None of them wanted the job of winching a dragon of that size (or indeed of any size) off the roof of Great Bootington Town Hall.

"Too risky," said one.

"Not if we don't know the weight," said another.

Several slammed down their phones in disbelief as soon as the word 'dragon' was uttered.

"We're not insured for dragons," said yet another.

The dragon remained.

"By heck," said Arthur. "What are we going to do? We've got to get rid of it before the Queen comes."

Mr Gorse shook his head mournfully. "Ee, I haven't a clue. The trouble is, if we don't get rid of it soon, the whole visit will be off."

"What?" cried Arthur. "But . . . all that money we've spent . . ."

"I know, I know. But it's the security risk, you see."

"How long have we got?" asked Arthur.

2

Floella Lends a Hand

In another part of Great Bootington, Floella was just setting out for the shops.

"I want to get all the washing done," said her father. "Get the cheapest you can of everything."

It was Wednesday so their hairdressing shop "Hairs and Graces" was closed. It was a very popular shop and customers came from all over Great Bootington for their trims, dyes and re-styling. Floella missed the bustle and excitement when it was closed. She missed talking to the three assistants and the various part-time helpers. She liked watching her father cutting and dyeing hair. He only did special customers who had to pay extra and he had lots of certificates and cups to show what a good hairdresser he was.

"Are we going to see Mum tonight?" she asked.

"Yes love."

Her mother was expecting a baby and she had to spend several weeks in hospital because she had a rare blood group and the doctors wanted to give her frequent check-ups.

Mr Jones came down the stairs carrying a pile of washing.

"And don't forget to buy some biscuits. Here."

Floella took the money and had a quick look at herself in the hall mirror. Her hair needed cutting, she thought, as she twisted the sleepers in her ears.

It was a hot day again so she wore a T-shirt, jeans and trainers. When she reached Library Street, she saw the seven traffic cones blocking off all the traffic. A policeman was there as well to stop crowds collecting. She went on down the street to Tescos which was not far from the Town Hall. Here she saw more cones and another policeman. Standing at the check-out five minutes later, she listened to the conversation of the two women in front of her.

"It's true. Sixteen firemen in hospital with dragon-poisoning," said one. "And two policemen, so they say, on the danger list."

The other woman looked disbelieving.

"But how did it get there?" she asked.

A man in front of them joined in.

"It's true, you know. I hear it's attacked three typists and it's cracked the roof of the Town Hall. The whole building might collapse."

The check-out girl was unmoved by all these comments.

"It's for the telly, I expect," she said. "One of those space films. It's not *real*."

Floella paid, loaded her goods into a shopping-bag and a carrier-bag and walked out. She might as well go and have a look although she thought they were probably talking a lot of nonsense. She remembered the time their next-door neighbour, Mrs Hodge, had woken them up in the middle of the night, screaming and carrying on about a lion with great staring eyes in her back yard. When Floella's Dad had

17

gone to have a look, carrying a monkey-wrench and a torch, it had turned out to be a stuffed owl on top of the dustbin. They never found out who had put it there. Probably this was just another daft joke.

She went into the Town Hall by a side door. There was no one about. She walked up the four flights of stairs, meeting only one man in a grey suit on the way. He was humming to himself and took no notice of her. She put the shopping-bags down in a room on the third floor. It said 'Committee Room 6' on the door.

On the floor below, Arthur and Mr Gorse were fending off requests from Granada TV to film the dragon from a helicopter, and questions from interested zookeepers all over the country and numerous cranks. As soon as they put any of the phones down, it rang again. The RSPCA, the Animal Liberation Front, Dragon's Lib and many other bodies, apart from numerous reporters, rang for information. Floella, oblivious to all the activity below her, stepped out onto the balcony where the walls and the floor were wet and blackened

18

with smoke.

Floella gazed at the dragon. It was the most beautiful she had ever seen. The sun glinted on its golden scales, jaws and tail. She started up the ladder, trying to keep a close watch on the dragon at the same time, just in case it moved.

She didn't walk straight up to its head. She first walked right round past the tail so she could see the other side of it. She noted the neat purple wing, the huge scaly body, the coiled tail, forked at the end, the huge claws (big as her hands). Then she noticed the other wing. It looked different. It sprawled away untidily onto the ground. More huge claws. She approached the head of the dragon which was sunk on the ground and stood, looking at it in admiration. It seemed to be asleep. She coughed.

The dragon opened one eye, then, when it saw Floella, it opened the other.

"Hello," she called. "I'm Floella."

"And what have you come to do to me?" asked the dragon. "Throw more water on me? Hurl pieces of card at me? Shout at me? What have I ever done to anyone to be treated like this?"

It had a clear musical voice and Floella wondered whether it was a he or a she dragon, but didn't like to ask. She decided it sounded more like a he.

"At least you said hello," the dragon went on. "No one else has uttered a word. They just assume I'm bad and try to get rid of me. It gives one a very poor view of human nature."

"I expect they're frightened," said Floella.

"Frightened?" said the dragon. "*They're* frightened? What about me? I'm hungry, lost and injured. But has anyone asked me? Did anyone ask me what I was doing here?"

"I tell you what," said Floella. "I'll get you something to eat. Then you can tell me the whole story."

The dragon broke into a smile and a short puff of smoke hovered over its head for a moment.

"Thank you Floella. That would be very welcome. I should like something to drink most. We dragons don't eat a lot once we're fully grown."

"I won't be long," said Floella. "I'll get

something out of my shopping bags. What's your name?"

"I can't tell you that," said the dragon. "Only other dragons may know my name and not all of those. But I can tell you that I am the Humzoala dragon of the Isle of Bight."

"Are you really?" said Floella. "That must be very grand. I'll be back soon."

She hurried down the ladder and back into the room where her shopping was. She had no idea what dragons ate. She took out some apples and two Crunchy bars.

Drink, she thought. She went off down the corridor and found what looked like a broom-cupboard.

"Hello young lady," said a smooth voice. "And what are you doing up here?"

Floella was startled to see in front of her, apparently sweeping the floor, a man with a perfectly bald head and a smooth pink face. From head to toe he looked quite unwrinkled and smooth. Even his clothes looked new and unworn. His voice sounded as if it had been ironed.

"I'm Mr Grubb the caretaker," he said as Floella remained silent. "Who let you in?"

3

Dragon in Danger

"I don't like that caretaker," Floella said a few minutes later as she watched the dragon swallow two Crunchy bars whole. She had stumped up and down several times with buckets of water for the dragon, some of which he had drunk. The rest she had used to bathe as much of his head and jaws as she could reach. "He wanted to know all about you but I didn't tell him anything – not that I know much. He said I shouldn't be in here really but he didn't stop me coming up. There's something fishy about him.'

The dragon winced as he tried to move his damaged right wing.

"There's something bad going on," he said.

"Someone tried to shoot me down. That's how I damaged my wing. With an arrow. There was someone on the island. Someone who didn't want me to leave."

"Why did you leave?" asked Floella. "You said you'd never left it before didn't you?"

She was sitting comfortably by the dragon's front legs.

"Danger," said the dragon. "I was warned of danger. The Duchess' seven-year-old daughter, Tamara, came to see me."

"What Duchess?" asked Floella.

The dragon sighed, exhaling puffs of grey smoke. Floella ducked.

"Don't you know anything? You've never spoken to a dragon before. You've never heard of the Isle of Bight or its Duchess. What on earth *do* you know?"

"Go on with your story," Floella said. "I can't help not knowing. We haven't done the British Isles in Geography yet. We're doing North America this year."

"What nonsense," muttered the dragon. "North America. Of what importance is that compared to the Isle of Bight? The island

24

is owned by the Duchess and Duke. Their daughter, Tamara, (and sometimes some of their other children) comes to talk and play with me. Now this is important. She wore a blue dress, white socks and blue sandals. As I was talking to her, rather we were singing in rounds I seem to remember, lo and behold I saw another little girl skipping up the hill towards me."

The dragon had a very long-winded way of telling a story thought Floella.

"Who?" she asked.

The dragon puffed a row of delicate white

smoke rings one after the other. They ascended vertically for about a metre and then floated away.

"I saw Tamara," said the dragon. "Wearing a blue dress, white socks and navy blue sandals."

"A twin sister?" asked Floella politely.

"No, no no," said the dragon. "When I saw the SECOND Tamara that's when I knew something was wrong. Something wicked was happening. There were *two* Tamaras."

Floella felt a bit sick. What if she saw another Floella walking towards her?

"What did you do?" she asked, wondering if the dragon was telling the truth.

"Fortunately," said the dragon, "the second Tamara hadn't seen the first one and vice versa. So I told the first one to hide and not to say a word. I had to confirm which was the real one."

"Go on," said Floella who was really interested now.

"The second little girl told me she had a message from her parents, the Duchess and Duke, that I should meet them on the Eastern Plains the next morning. I said I would be there. As soon as she skipped off, I asked the first one, who was very frightened, to run home as fast as she could. She was to ask her parents if they had sent me any message. (I was sure, you see, that she was the *real* Tamara). If they had not, she was to fly a red flag from the chimney of the house. I can see it easily from the Blue Hill."

"And then?"

"Only half an hour later a red flag was flown from the chimney," said the dragon. "The other child (whom I already suspected because she didn't address me as 'Humzo' as the real Tamara always did) was a cantrip of Miss Squidger, a bad magician. She has made many evil spells and charms in the past and it is well known she steals children and others from the island and binds them to serve her. I knew at once that, for some reason which I could not tell, she had designs on me. I was uncertain what to do. I am the last of my line. As I have no other dragons to turn to on the island, I thought about it all night and decided to fly to the mainland early this morning.

27

I was hoping to find friends who would help uncover the evil schemes of Miss Squidger and her cronies. But alas, just as I started to fly away across the May Strait, someone drew a bow and arrow and tried to shoot me down. Not to kill me, I think, but to stop me leaving."

The dragon gave a shuddering gasp and Floella suddenly realised in how much pain it really was.

"I struggled on with just one wing working properly and managed to descend, not without great bruising and laceration, onto this . . . this . . ."

"Roof," said Floella.

"But I am wounded and friendless," said the dragon, "and she will be sending her spies out to look for me. They may even be here already. If she went to the trouble of shape-turning, then certainly she wanted me alive . . . but what for, I cannot imagine."

"I'll be your friend," said Floella.

"Hm," said the dragon. "But what can you do? I've got to leave here before she finds me."

"They're all trying to think of ways to

28

get you off," said Floella. "All the people in the Town Hall. They're worried you'll crack the roof. And there's the Queen's visit on Thursday."

"If they think pouring water on me helps, the people here must be far more stupid than those on the Isle of Bight," said the dragon.

"Are you sure your wing's broken?" asked Floella. "It must have been badly shaken but unless the bone's broken . . ."

"Bone?" said the dragon. "Bone? I don't have just one bone in my wing you know. There are three dozen at least."

"Let me have a look anyway," said Floella. She looked first at the good left wing. "Could you sort of stretch this one so I can look at it?"

Grudgingly the dragon did so. Studying it, Floella could see that the wing was composed of several pieces, each containing a bone. The large pieces near to the dragon's body tapered to about her arm's length at the off-side. She touched the part of the wing on the ground. It felt scratchy. The bone felt thick and strong like seasoned purple wood. Then she walked round and examined the other one carefully.

"You haven't broken any of the larger
bones," she said. "And as far as I can
see, you've just splintered a small bone and
there's a hole in your scales. That makes the
end part of your wing droop so you can't keep
your balance. If we could stick up the splinter
and add something strong to it and then fill
the hole, it might be all right."

"Really?" said the dragon. "I thought I'd
broken a major bone at least."

"Not as far as I can tell," said Floella.
"It's hard to see. You're so big."

"Nonsense," said the dragon. "You're so

small. Anyway, what can be done about it? It's only a matter of time before Miss Squidger catches up with me."

"I'll think of something," said Floella, "but I'll have to go home now. My Dad'll be wondering where I am. I'll come back as soon as I can. See you."

The dragon gave a little puff of smoke and shut its great red eyes. Floella took a bus home because she knew she was already late. After she and her father had made their dinner, she went round to see her friend Seb. She found him in the garden feeding his rabbits and guinea-pigs.

"Hi Seb."

"Hi," said Seb. He was holding a fluffy white rabbit under his arm. He was a short wiry boy with brown hair and tortoiseshell spectacles. He had lost so many pairs that now he always carried a spare pair in his pocket.

"Why are you doing that?" Floella asked as he set the rabbit down on the lawn. "Won't it run away?"

"No," laughed Seb. "Not with all the free

food she gets. She's really tame."

"Have you ever had any pet birds?" Floella asked.

"Why?" asked Seb. "I didn't think you were interested in stuff like that."

"No," said Floella. "We haven't got the space for pets really. But have you got a bird?"

"I once had a sparrow with a sore foot," said Seb. "I looked after it and fed it until it got better. It was a bit difficult though with Zanzibar."

Zanzibar, a sleek black-and-white cat, strolled onto the lawn and sat down beside the rabbit. They began a mock boxing-match together.

"It didn't have a broken wing then?" asked Floella.

"Look, what is this?" asked Seb. "Have you got a poorly parrot or a vomiting vulture?"

"You won't believe this," began Floella.

4

Mending Bones

Later on that day, Seb and Floella were making
their way on Seb's mother's bike towards the
Town Hall. Floella sat on the carrier above the
back wheel while in the front basket was an
array of material Seb thought might be useful
– Superglue, Instant-Set Polyfilla, balsa rods,
chicken wire, some pieces of wood he'd found
in the greenhouse, a ball of twine and some
scissors.

"If it's some sort of practical joke," he said
as they waited at the traffic-lights opposite the
Fit-Ezi shoe shop, "I'll push your face in."

"If you ever watched telly," said Floella,
"instead of spending all your time cleaning
out fishtanks and rabbit-hutches you'd prob-

ably have seen something about it."

"O.K."

"Jings," said Floella as they set off again behind a dawdling doubledecker bus, "if it's on the telly, that Miss Squidger might already have found out where he is – that's if they have the telly on the Isle of Bight."

They arrived and Seb chained the bike to the railings.

"There's no one about now," said Floella. "There were loads this morning."

"Can we just go in?" Seb asked, looking doubtfully up at the Town Hall.

"Why not?" said Floella. "I did this morning. Come on. I just hope we don't bump into that horrible caretaker."

She was disappointed, for on the fourth floor Mr Grubb oozed towards them.

"Are you going to see the Humzoala dragon?" he asked, stretching his lips into a smile.

"How d'you know it's a Humzoala Dragon?" asked Floella.

Mr Grubb's smile broadened and he nodded his head.

"Shall we say a little bird told me, someone

who's interested in its whereabouts?"

"You mean Miss Squidger I suppose?" Seb said airily as if he knew all about it. "We're representing the *Others*."

"Really?" said Mr Grubb, rubbing his smooth pale hands together and staring at the children with bulging brown eyes. "Of course I'm ready to help anyone, provided," he coughed, "we understand each other. Certainly Miss Squidger is hoping I'll be able to recover her dragon . . ."

"It's *not* hers," put in Floella fiercely.

"Of course I take no sides."

"You will be well rewarded by the Others," said Seb, "if you help us."

"A ladder," said Floella. "We need a ladder."

Mr Grubb disappeared soft-footed, to return with a folding ladder. He declined to help them up to the roof with it however and disappeared into the broom cupboard.

"Whatever did you say all that for about the 'Others'?" asked Floella. "I think he's some kind of wizard in league with Miss Squidger. I don't believe he's a caretaker at all."

"He may be a wizard," said Seb, "but I think he's on anyone's side as long as they're winning."

"But he'll go off and tell her," said Floella. "He may have some method of communicating with her. She'll know all about us."

"Not all," said Seb. "She won't know who the Others are. I bet that'll worry her."

Floella kicked the skirting-board. She felt it was a mistake to let Mr Grubb know anything.

"Come on then," she said. "Let's get the ladder up."

"Superb," said Seb when at last he could see the dragon fully. "What a beautiful creature."

The dragon opened one red eye. "I thought you were never coming," he said. "Have you got anything to drink?"

"O.K., I'll get you some," sighed Floella. "This is Seb. Seb, this is the Humzoala Dragon. He's come to mend your wing."

"Not mend exactly," said Seb nervously, "just sort of patch it up."

He set up the ladder by the side of the dragon and waited for Floella to come back.

When she had been up and down three times with water he began to get cross.

"Look, that Squidger knows where you are. She's probably thinking of a scheme to get hold of you right this minute. You'll just have to wait if you want any more water. Floella, can you hold the ladder steady and pass me up some things?"

Seb stood at the top of the ladder with some Superglue and balsa wood. The dragon grumbled and twitched.

"I think that splint will hold. Now we've

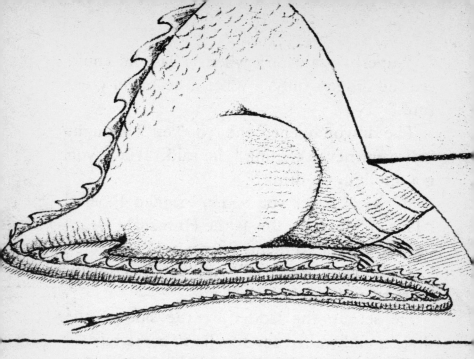

got to do something about this hole." Together
they mixed up some Polyfilla in a bucket.

"Here, we can do this together," she
said. "We can reach it from here." They
slapped it on, superglueing some balsa wood
and chickenwire on either side of it to keep it
in place while it hardened.

"Now," said Floella to the dragon, "try
and see if you can move it up and down a
bit."

They watched anxiously as the dragon carefully extended its wings.

"It seems all right," said Seb, "except for a bit right up at the top. Here Floella. Help me. We'll have to crawl out over his back."

Floella stepped off the ladder onto the dragon's back, carefully avoiding the mended parts. She and Seb crawled as best they could to the top of the wing and applied some more balsa wood and Polyfilla.

Just as they called to the dragon to try his wings, there was a tremendous commotion and Mr Grubb burst onto the roof shouting, "They're coming with a crane to lift it off," and at the same time they heard, much nearer, a strange whirring noise.

Slowly, the dragon stretched his wings. Seb and Floella held their breath as the mended wing extended itself, then hung on for dear life as the dragon flapped both wings vigorously up and down.

"Might have waited for us to find a safe place," grumbled Floella.

Worse was to follow. Without a word of warning, the dragon, having found the wing in suitable condition, swivelled round and made a rapid vertical take-off. Seb and Floella hung on as best they could to the scales on its neck. As they gained height, the shouting, whirring and screaming from below was soon left far behind.

5

Isle of Bight Secrets

On the Isle of Bight, separated from the west coast of Britain by the May Strait, Miss Squidger was staring through the window into her garden where rows of flowers stood to attention in carefully-gradated rows. Scum, her dog, a cross between a Chow and a Dobermann Pinscher, lay on the grass, eyeing malevolently everything that moved. Miss Squidger was thin and long with thin long feet and spiky hair the colour of tapioca. Her eyes were the hue of dishwater with the glint of polished steel.

Pogglow, her crony, sat on a stool nearby, polishing up a crystal ball. He made up in breadth what he lacked in height. Dressed in a tight red velvet knickerbocker suit from which buttons were always popping, yellow socks and white suede shoes with cuban heels, Pogglow looked like a garden gnome with chronic indigestion. His greatest asset, in the eyes of Miss Squidger, although she was careful not to let him know this, was that he was a human truth drug. Due to some peculiarity in his genetic make-up, he responded in a singular manner to direct statements. If they were false he glowed all over, his skin exuding an unmistakable orange light. If someone expressed an opinion or what they thought to be true, there was no glow. If the person lied deliberately, he glowed.

Pogglow himself, was entirely unaware when he glowed. He attributed Miss Squidger's apparent devotion to his keen brain and handsome appearance. Miss Squidger, for her part, prevented other people from noticing his peculiarity by persuading him to cover as much of himself as possible. In public, she ordered him to wear white leather gloves and a hat with a brim and a curling feather pulled well over his face so that he looked a very odd

figure indeed.

"The time is ripe, Pogglow," Miss Squidger said. "Soon I shall be able to have what I've plotted for – the ownership of the Isle of Bight. The time has almost come for the Duchess and Duke to renew the lease for another nine hundred and ninety-nine years. If they can't afford to do so, and it's common knowledge that they are practically penniless, having squandered all their fortune on their enormous family and in giving money away to every Jill, Pat and Mary, then . . ." she paused and snapped her fingers in triumph.

Pogglow creased his fat face into a smile. "Then the island goes on the open market," he said. "But where will the money . . .?"

"Aha," interrupted Miss Squidger. "You've heard of the Isle of Bight sapphires Pogglow?" She didn't wait for an answer but went on, "These sapphires belong to the ruling Bight family, ancestors of the present Duchess, but although they have been in the family for hundreds of years their present whereabouts is not known. My crystal ball tells me that these cornflower-blue sapphires, originally from Kashmir, larger and more precious than any other sapphires in the entire world, are not lost irrecoverably. They have been hidden and their whereabouts may yet be discovered, even though," her voice sank to a whisper, "even though, Pogglow, the present Duchess and Duke themselves do not know where they are."

Pogglow watched her expectantly.

"What is more, there is one creature on this island who can tell me where they are hidden." She cackled with pleasure. "Once we have those Pogglow, the island is mine."

Her hands closed on a piece of paper lying on her table and crushed it exultantly. Then her nails shredded the paper into tiny pieces.

"But who . . . what is the creature?" asked Pogglow.

"Aha. That's even more interesting," Miss Squidger said. "This creature does not even *know* it has the knowledge. It has been transmitted through its kind for generations but it lies at a deep level of its brain. It can only be brought to the surface by drugs or hypnosis. Traditionally, these creatures have been protectors of the Bight family treasures."

She pressed a bell on the table and a pale girl wearing an apron over a dingy dress entered, carrying a tray with hot drinks and a plate of biscuits. Her face was red round the eyes and nostrils.

She placed the tray on the table and turned to go.

"Wait, Sparrow," said Miss Squidger. She looked suspiciously at the plate of biscuits. "There aren't many. Have you been eating them?"

She watched Pogglow as Sparrow answered,

"No, I haven't."

He remained pale and Miss Squidger was satisfied.

"Very well Sparrow. See if Grubb has returned yet from his message to the Humzoala Dragon." When Sparrow had left, she said, "Yes, it's the Humzoala Dragon who knows where the sapphires are. Let me see, Pogglow, where exactly on this island do these creatures live?"

"There is only one now Miss Squidger, the last of the line, or so my mother always told me as a child. It lives on the western side of the Island. On the Blue Hill, near . . . near the Moonberry Tree."

"Silence," rasped Miss Squidger, smashing her fist onto the table so that the cups and plates rattled. Pogglow, fat and stodgy as he was, was startled.

The Moonberry Tree had stood on the Isle of Bight since time out of mind. Some said it had been there before the Island and its roots led through the Island to the sea below. It was held in great respect by all the inhabitants. Many were the remarkable happenings reported to have taken place beneath its peaceful shade. Many festivals and holidays had been celebrated around its gracious boughs. The only festival of note now surviving was the Moonberry Morris Dance Day which took place every year at the autumnal equinox.

Miss Squidger therefore, who wished to control and have power over everyone, hated and feared the tree. She scowled as Sparrow re-entered the room alone.

"He hasn't come back," faltered Sparrow. "He sent this letter." Miss Squidger snatched it and ripped it open.

"What?" she screeched as she read it. "Pogglow. Bring the crystal ball. You get out."

Sparrow fled.

Miss Squidger passed her hands over the crystal and peered intently into it. "Ah," she said after a few minutes. "There's Grubb. Close the curtains, Pogglow. Quick, you buffoon."

In his haste, Pogglow banged his head on the table. Miss Squidger passed her hands again over the crystal. After about twenty seconds

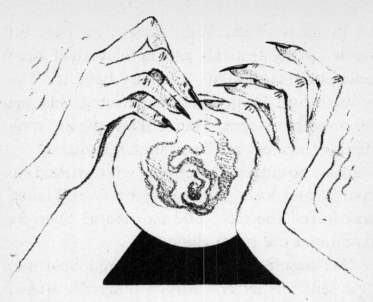

the pictures faded and she threw a dark cloth over it.

"Stop rubbing your head, you nincom-poop," she said to Pogglow, "and listen. The dragon has left the island and Grubb has gone in pursuit. It's quite unknown for the dragon, or any of its ancestors to leave the island so it must have suspected danger. If I find there has been *treachery* in this," she went on in a tone which frizzled every hair on Pogglow's head, "I shall seek out the traitor and punish him, her or it." Pogglow shivered. "Now, we must hurry." She pressed the bell once more.

"Sparrow," she said as soon as the girl appeared. "Send the helicopter pilot and his mate to me at once."

Miss Squidger ground her teeth and kicked at the table impatiently until two men in red boiler suits appeared.

She explained to them very carefully exactly what she wanted them to do. "There is absolutely no danger," she said firmly, "but you must hurry. Just do precisely what I have told you. Pogglow, give them everything they need quickly."

Before they left, Miss Squidger made them repeat their instructions to her.

"Excellent," she said. "You have all you need. Go quickly and don't come back till your mission is accomplished."

6

Escape to Upper Goolash

At Great Bootington Town Hall, the onlookers stared, flabbergasted, as the dragon shot upwards. The crane-driver in his little cab, who had come to take a preliminary look, wondered briefly if it was a telly commercial and then returned to ground level to have a cup of tea. Arthur watched from the safety of the Town Hall balcony while typists, secretaries, cashiers, accountants and other assorted flotsam hanging from every available window in order to watch the crane operation, now saw the dragon become a dot and then disappear entirely from view.

"Funny," said Maisie as she drew her head in. "Thought I saw something moving on its back, did you?"

Everyone was so occupied in watching the departing dragon that they did not at first notice either the sight or the sound of the sludge-coloured helicopter which had landed on the Town Hall roof shortly afterwards.

"Hey," said Arthur, "don't remember anyone booking a helicopter. Are they with Craneco?"

No one knew.

"Who's that man there?" he went on. The figure of Mr Grubb could be seen talking to the pilot of the helicopter. "How did he get up there?" He sent a man to speak to Craneco and asked a nearby policeman to check the man out. "Can't be too careful with the Queen's visit coming up," he said. "Might be some loony."

The helicopter took off with an angry snarl of its engine while the puzzled Craneco men prepared to leave. The foreman was busy voicing his opinion on Great Bootington Council, practical jokes, dragons and town halls with flat roofs.

"Off our beat now," said Arthur philosophically as he went down the stairs. "Wonder where it went?"

"Let us hope not to another Town Hall roof," said Mr Singh.

"Nay," said Maisie. "None of them's daft enough to have a flat one."

They all laughed and went back to their respective duties.

"Ee, went a fair lick did that," said the man who had been hoisted up in the crane. "Who were those two kids on board then?"

"What?" said a bystander. "Children? Are you sure? What were they doing on the roof?"

A few minutes later Town Hall officials learned to their consternation that the matter of the dragon could not, as they had hoped, be forgotten.

"The creature must be tracked down," it was declared, "and charged with kidnapping." Meanwhile it was hoped that Mr Grubb, who had been taken into custody for questioning, might be able to throw some light on the matter.

Meanwhile Seb and Floella were enduring

the most uncomfortable ride of their lives. The dragon's body was hard and slippery and there wasn't anything comfortable to hang onto.

"The wing's mended at any rate," shouted Floella. It seemed very noisy up in the air.

Seb grunted. "Only temporary," he said. "It might come unstuck at any moment."

"Worryguts," said Floella. "I don't want to know that. Aaarrrgghhhh".

Floella grabbed Seb as he lurched forward and almost fell off into bare sky.

"Hold on you idiot." He sat down with a bump and they clutched each other in alarm.

"My glasses," cried Seb. "They've fallen off. I've lost them." He felt in his jeans pocket. "Thank goodness I've got a spare pair."

"Well don't put them on now," Floella said sharply, "or you'll lose them too. Wait till we land."

"Land? But where? Does he even know where he's going?"

"I don't suppose so," said Floella, "especially if he's never left the island before."

"Then what's the point?" asked Seb crossly. "I thought he was going for help."

"I don't know," said Floella, "but did you see, there was a helicopter landed on the roof just after we took off. I wonder who it was."

"Ssh," said Seb and suddenly they heard a fierce humming, grinding sound. It grew louder and soon they could see in the distance the outline of a helicopter.

"It's following us," said Floella. The dragon, aware of danger, put himself into top gear. They rushed through the air with such speed that all Floella and Seb could do was cling on. Still they could hear the hum of the helicopter.

Then they found themselves unable to see anything as they rushed past, even if there'd been time to look at it. They were enveloped in thick fog. It was like flying through a thick wodge of cottonwool. They could hear and see nothing.

"At least the helicopter will lose us now," Floella whispered.

Seb was silent. He was wondering if the dragon could tell (if it had ever known) where it was going and whether they might not crash into something which the dragon wouldn't be able to see until it was too late. On and on they flew through the fog which was not only thick and quiet but also cold. Soon they became aware that they were slowing down and losing height. The dragon was flying erratically and its right wing was drooping a little. then it seemed to make a tremendous effort to descend gradually, until it was slowly circling round and round. Floella couldn't make out the outline of any houses or trees or lamp posts, so thick was the fog.

"Let's hope we're not going to land on another roof," she said to Seb.

"Or in the middle of a motorway," Seb said, "but I don't think so. I can't hear any noise."

Indeed it was remarkably quiet. As they circled round again in an even lower sweep, there was a bump and a jolt so that they were rammed hard into the dragon's sharp scales and then they were at rest. Floella and Seb climbed cautiously down. They were cold, scratched and bruised. They could see nothing. Thick fog loomed all round. As they sat, shivering, the fog began slowly to clear.

At first the shadows, then the tall bushes themselves, began to be visible. All around them stretched flat marsh dotted with coarse tussocks of grass and small spiky plants. A few stunted trees huddled together. Not far from where they had landed was a notice saying 'Beware dangerous marshes'. We nearly landed there, Floella thought. She turned and saw in front of them land which looked like a football field on which six games had been played one after the other in the pouring rain. In the distance, about a quarter of a mile away, a few small houses could be seen.

On a tree a chipped notice was nailed. WELCOME TO UPPER GOOLASH it said.

7

The Healer

"Not much of a welcome," said Floella staring at the bare marshy ground.

"He doesn't look very well either," whispered Seb nodding towards the dragon. The dragon's right wing was drooping and his great head rested on the ground, his eyes closed. He didn't move.

"No one seems to live here," said Floella. "We must have landed here because he ran out of puff. I thought he had somewhere definite in mind when he took off."

Seb looked up. "Anyone for miles around can see us," he said.

"Especially from the sky," said Floella and they both thought of but did not mention the sludge-coloured helicopter.

"You stay here with the dragon," Floella said. "I'll see if I can get help. Somebody must live in Upper Goolash and we definitely can't get away from here until the dragon's had his wing attended to."

"O.K.," said Seb.

She reached the stubby trees and then made her way to the small scattering of houses. The grass was still damp from the fog but a faint sun could now be seen. There was no sign of people, animals or birds. Then as she walked on she came to a handful of cottages, a small post-office and general shop and a garage with two petrol pumps. Further on there were a few more cottages and the Upper Goolash Arms. A sign-post said "Penrith Holmes 3 miles". There was no sign of Lower Goolash. Perhaps it had sunk into the marshes long ago. She hesitated in front of the cottages, not knowing what to do. It didn't look as if she would find a vet or doctor here. She caught sight of a thin black cat treading delicately through a line of collapsed bricks to the back of one of the cottages. Floella followed it, simply because she liked cats. It

darted through the back door of an old but
trimly-kept cottage. As Floella rapped on the
open door she could smell something cooking
and she suddenly realised how long it was since
she had eaten.

"Come in," said a voice. "I thought there
were strangers here." A man who was the
oldest person she had ever seen stood in the
doorway. His face was criss-crossed with little
creases like a much-folded map. He had white
hair which reached to his shoulders and a white
beard. Even his eyebrows and eyelashes were
white. He wore an old tweed suit and pink
carpet slippers. His voice was quavery and

went from gruff to squeaky and back again.

Floella followed him inside and sat down on a stool near the big wood stove on which stood several pots. The man sat down opposite her, first placing before her a mug of tea and a plate of rabbit stew.

"Help yourself to bread," he said. "I'm the Healer. I make pills and potions for people who can't find or don't want a doctor."

"What people?" asked Floella. "Not many people seem to live here."

"Look there," said the Healer, motioning to the window. "D'you see that hill?"

Floella nodded, her mouth full of the stew (which was very tasty indeed).

"On the other side of that hill lies Penrith Holmes," he said. "A lot of people lived here once but now most have moved out and up there. It was too old-fashioned here for them but they still want the Healer, all the same."

"Why don't you go and live there too?" asked Floella.

"I'm quite happy here," sniffed the Healer. "There's a good shop and a post-office and a pub. Anyway Spadger and I are used to these marshes. We were born here and will die here, I dare say."

I suppose Spadger's the cat thought Floella.

"Where have you come from?" asked the Healer, "and how did you get here? Where are you going to stay tonight?"

Floella looked at her watch and realised that it was nearly six o'clock.

"I'm from Great Bootington and so is my friend but . . ."

"Great Bootington? Really? That *is* good news. I have a very good friend there, Jeremiah Gorse. I'm sure you'd not mind taking a message to him?"

"No, said Floella, "but we can't get back there till you've healed the dragon."

"Dragon?" gruffed the Healer as his voice came out suddenly low. "So you came by dragon?"

"Yes," said Floella. "He came from the Isle of Bight. He's hurt his wing."

"Goodnessome Goodnessomy. Did you say the Isle of Bight? What a coincidence!"

"Yes," said Floella impatiently. She'd never get away at this rate.

62

"Never mind child. We'll come back to that. First of all now, which wing? Whereabouts? What size dragon? How old? Are any bones broken? Has any treatment been given?"

Floella started to answer the questions as best as she could one by one. As she did so, the Healer took out various bottles and packets from a wall-cupboard.

"Mm," he said, deftly measuring a drop here, a twist of powder there and mixing them carefully with a glass rod. "Well it's not much to go on. I prefer to see the patient first when at all possible." He squeaked suddenly into a higher note. "But there isn't time." He heated the mixture gently in a tiny saucepan and then poured it through a funnel into a jar.

"Oh dear, oh dear, oh Goodnessome, oh Goodnessoyou," he muttered to himself. "The dragon-healing cream. There's a vital ingredient missing. I'll have to go into Penrith Holmes for it."

"How long will that take?" asked Floella. "We must leave here as quickly as possible. It's very urgent. Wouldn't that stuff in the bottle be all right on its own?"

"No no no," said the Healer. "No no no. Without the cream, the wing might suddenly c-r-u-m-b-l-e in mid-air, just like that. Are you coming with me?"

"I might as well," said Floella who thought she might be able to hurry him up a bit if she was with him, although he didn't seem a hurrying sort of person.

The Healer told Spadger where he was going and went out, leaving the door open. He threw a voluminous fur coat round his shoulders.

As they walked up the hill the Healer told Floella all about the history of Upper Goolash and Penrith Holmes, about his childhood on the Isle of Bight with his sister with whom he had had a bitter quarrel. Floella wondered if she was as old as he was.

In Penrith Holmes, which was a flourishing small town, very different from Upper Goolash, the Healer was greeted by many people. He found the ingredients he wanted in an old-fashioned chemist's shop in the market square. By the time the Healer was ready to return, Floella was fretting with impatience. Were dragons very strong, she wondered.

She petted Spadger while she waited for the Healer to make up the dragon-healing cream and write a letter to his old friend.

"But I can't pay you," she said just as she was about to leave, ashamed to realise she hadn't thought of it before.

"That's all right," the Healer said, squeaking up the scale again. "You're doing me a great favour by taking that letter to my old friend. By the way, if you and your friend Seb need somewhere to sleep tonight, you can always stop here."

"Thank you," said Floella, "but we're in a great hurry."

"We'll see," smiled the Healer. "But promise me one thing, that you'll give that letter to my friend at the very earliest moment that you can when you get back to Great Bootington. I suspect he can help you."

Floella nodded and hurried off. She ran most of the way back. She had just reached the six stunted trees when she heard the noise of the helicopter. She broke into a run but as she approached, she realised the helicopter was not landing. It was taking off.

She was too late.

8

The Question

When Floella had gone, Seb began to look at
the dragon's wing but had nothing with him
to patch it up a bit more. Then just as he was
looking in his pockets for something to eat, he
heard a loud noise above him. The helicopter
had caught up with them at last. Seb crouched
at the side of the dragon's right leg with his
hands over his ears as the machine whirred
menacingly over them. Then it descended so
suddenly that at first he felt sure it was going to
land right on top of the dragon. But it didn't. It
landed about ten yards away. There was a thud
and a screech and then complete silence.

The dragon didn't move which worried Seb
very much. At last the door of the helicopter

opened and out stepped the pilot dressed in a red boiler-suit. He marched straight up to the dragon, stopping within two yards of it. Seb stayed where he was. The pilot stood still in front of the dragon and began to speak slowly:

"Greetings O Humzoala Dragon. Greetings."

At this the Humzoala Dragon lifted its massive head and opened its magnificent blood red eyes. The pilot took out a red and green rubber ball from an inside pocket, talking all the time. He began to bounce the ball so that it reached right up to the top of the dragon's head.

"O great and gracious dragon, I am honoured to meet you. I have travelled day and night through fog and wind to have this honour."

As he spoke, he bounced the ball and caught it and bounced it again and caught it, time after time in front of the dragon.

Seb stealthily moved from under the dragon's foot and watched. Then he saw what was happening. The pilot was trying to mesmerize the dragon, lulling him with the slow, steady bouncing of the ball. While he did this, anoth-

er man was creeping round to the left. Now he was erecting a collapsible stepladder. No sooner had he done this than he bounded up the steps and stood on the small platform at the top. All the time the pilot was bouncing the ball and talking in his monotonous chant to the dragon. Meanwhile the man on the platform suddenly raised his arm and before Seb could cry out (which wouldn't have done any good anyway) sent a long silver spear hissing through the air. It pierced the dragon's soft stomach where it was unprotected by scales. The dragon collapsed and rolled over, its head lolling on the ground. Fortunately for Seb, the dragon collapsed onto the opposite side to which he was crouching or he would certainly have been crushed to death. Seb waited to see what would happen next. Would they find him and kill him as well? Then at the first words of the two men he felt a little bit more hopeful.

"The drug takes a little while to work," said the pilot. "He'll be asleep for about twenty minutes." (He's not dead, thought Seb joyfully). "Then when he wakes up we ask him the question. It's a truth drug, see. He's bound to tell us the right answer, according to Squidger." At least I'll hear it too, thought Seb, as long as I keep quiet. The two men sat down on the ground quite near to the dragon.

"Could do with something to eat Gaz," said the pilot. "No joke going through all that fog. No danger, she said. All right for her just sitting there giving orders. Wonder what happened to those kids Grubb said were on board?"

"Probably fell off and got sucked into the marshes," said Gaz. "Don't worry about them. What about something to eat though, eh Baz?"

"Doesn't look as if there's a Wimpy or a Kentucky Fried round here."

Gaz almost exploded with laughter at this. He shook all over and slapped his arms and legs. He coughed and spluttered and wheezed till Baz thumped him on the back.

"That's a good one," he said when at last he could speak. "Wimpy or Kentucky Fried . . ." he dissolved into great gasping roars of laughter again.

Baz took no notice. He was feeling in all his pockets. Next he took off his safety helmet.

"Here we are," he said, producing a packet sellotaped to the inside. "That Sparrow girl gave them to me." He unwrapped it to reveal two Cornish pasties and a pork pie.

After they'd eaten they sat still, gradually falling asleep until suddenly the dragon shivered, lashed its great forked tail and awoke.

Baz and Gaz almost leapt out of their skins.

"Quick Gaz. Now get up the stepladder."

"No," said Gaz. "You've got that bit wrong Baz."

"Eh?"

"Not me, *us*. I'm not doing this on my own, remember. We both have to ask it together. Then it'll sleep for twelve hours or so while we make a quick getaway."

"No lad, I drive. You do the heavies."

"No," said Gaz. "When it comes to dragons, we're in it together or not at all."

"O.K. then. Let's get it over with. There's a wind starting up."

The two men climbed up the ladder and looked into the dragon's huge blood red eyes.

"Greetings o honoured and respected dragon," they chanted together, looking at the piece of paper with their instructions.

The dragon was silent.

"We have come to seek your help o great and glorious dragon, the last in the line of Humzoala Dragons."

The dragon appeared to be listening intently.

"We seek your reply to an important question."

Silence.

Baz and Gaz were sweating. Were they doing it right? What if the dragon didn't answer the question? What if it didn't know the answer as Miss Squidger said it did? How could a dragon talk anyway?

"You ready Gaz? This is it."

"Right you are then."

They cleared their throats and began:

"O glorious and magnificent Humzoala Dragon, greetings to you. We beg you to answer our question: where are the Isle of Bight sapphires?"

There was a deep silence.

Even the wind seemed to stop blowing for a moment while, close against the dragon's side,

Seb held his breath.

"O glorious and magnificent Humzoala Dragon," Baz and Gaz began again (Miss Squidger had told them they could ask three times and after the third time the dragon would have to answer it if it had not done so before), "greetings to you. We beg you to answer our question: where are the Isle of Bight sapphires?"

Silence.

As Baz and Gaz concentrated all their attention on the dragon, Seb pinched his nose to stop himself from sneezing.

After a suitable silence, Baz and Gaz began for the third time: "O glorious and magnificent Humzoala Dragon, greetings to you. We beg you to answer our question: where are the Isle of Bight sapphires?"

Another deep silence. Then a puff of smoke emerged from the dragon's nostrils and floated upwards in a series of perfectly-formed rings.

At last the dragon spoke,

"The Bight sapphires are no longer on the Isle of Bight. They were removed to Great Bootington by the twenty-first Duchess."

Another series of smoke rings after this
showed that the pronouncement was at an end.
Seb had hardly taken in this astonishing news
before Baz and Gaz were folding up their ladder and making for the helicopter. As it sped
off the dragon rolled to one side, his head flat
on the ground and his tail, discoloured with
dust, flopped limply.

9

The Duchess has a Visitor

Meanwhile the Duchess and Duke of Bight were sitting in their crumbling three-storeyed house. It was breakfast-time and the whole family was sitting in the large kitchen on the first floor.

"Only three days," said the Duchess, a lovely fat woman who wore flowered baggy trousers, tunic and matching turban. "What are we going to do Platto?"

The Duke's name was Plantaganet but the Duchess always called him Platto except when she was cross.

Platto, thin and tall and nervous, finished his scrambled eggs and bacon and had a sip of decaffeinated coffee.

"And I hear Miss Squidger is going to put in a bid for the island. At least that's what that poor Sparrow girl told Tamara. And we have to think of the other people on the island, Platto. She'll do terrible things if she manages to get control of it. She's already stolen children from the village, although no one will admit to anything, they're so afraid of her."

"We've got to find those sapphires," the Duke said again, standing up and brushing the crumbs off his T-shirt. "We know they're not in this house. We've searched every corner of it. Besides, the children would have found them if we hadn't."

They had just finished washing up and tidying everything away when there was a loud bang at the front door. The Duke stuck his head out of the window to make sure it wasn't someone come to ask for money.

"Who is it?" asked the Duchess.

"I don't know," said the Duke. "I've never seen him before. He's carrying a camera and an overnight bag."

"I'll go," said the Duchess. She went slowly downstairs to the front door. In the hall Bottom was attacking a packet of raw fishfingers he'd snatched from the fridge. She stepped over him and opened the door.

"Hi there," said the tall man in a safari suit and peaked cap who stood on the doorstep. "You have a real swell house here ma'am, real swell."

"Thank you," said the Duchess. "We like it."

"Let me introduce myself. I'm Elmer T. Pinewood Junior of Florence."

"Florence in Italy?" asked the Duchess excitedly for she had always wanted to visit Italy.

"No ma'am, Oregon, the United States of A. Am I right in thinking you're the Duchess of this beautiful island?"

"Yes indeed," beamed the Duchess. "Do come in and meet my husband Mr Pinewood."

"Call me Elmer. Elmer will be just dandy, Duchess."

"This is Elmer, Elmer T. Pinewood my dear," said the Duchess to the surprised Duke who was just getting down to the Guardian crossword.

"Junior".

"We've got to find those sapphires, Hermione," he said. "Then we'd have plenty of money."

Rosalind, Viola, Olivia and Perdita all started talking at once:

"Can I get down?"

"Can I have some more toast?"

"My fried egg's got spiders on."

"Why can't we have a video recorder?"

At the same time Hamlet began to cry because Tamara had pinched him and Portia, Touchstone and Romeo began to fight over the plastic toy in the Krispiecrunchoes packet. Antonio, at three the baby of the family, sat happily on a rug chewing the leg of his teddy-bear, Flat Harry. Shylock started to bark loudly and Bottom the cat, seizing her opportunity, leaped onto the table and dragged off the Duchess' kipper.

At last order was restored with the help of Beatrice, their sole remaining servant, who took all of them except Bottom off to the park with her.

"It's dreadful," said the Duchess, mopping up her tears with a kitchen cloth. "What shall we do Platto? We need more servants."

"I know, my sugarplum," said the Duke soothingly, patting the Duchess on her turban, "but where's the money to come from? Look at all these unpaid bills." He pointed to a pile of papers reaching right up to the ceiling. "We have to pay all these besides renewing the lease. If we don't find the money, we'll lose our home, everything."

"Mr Elmer T. Pinewood *Junior*," said the Duchess. "He's come . . ." She paused. Why had he come? Perhaps he was really another debt-collector or a spy sent by Miss Squidger.

Mr Elmer T. Pinewood Junior gazed with pleasure round the kitchen.

"I guess this is an original old English kitchen," he said. "Real quaint. Now, let me explain why I'm here. I'm interested in precious stones. I'm a jeweller. Doing pretty well. Have a string of shops on the go back in Oregon. Now I believe you own some very famous sapphires."

The Duke jumped up. "How did you know about the sapphires?" he asked. "Who told you? How did you know where to come?"

Elmer T. Pinewood didn't seem a bit put out by the Duke's manner. "Why," he said, pulling a small leather book out of his pocket, "from Jacob Tuttle's 'Precious Stones of Europe' 1963, revised and amended 1989."

"You mean they're famous?" said the Duchess.

"That's right ma'am," said Elmer, looking wistfully round the kitchen. "Gee that's a real pretty tea-service. I'd sure like to try some of your real English tea."

At that moment Beatrice appeared with Shylock who bounded up to Elmer and leapt onto his lap.

"Beatrice, could you make Mr Pinewood some tea?" asked the Duchess, "In fact we'll all have some. And some cakes," she added, for she was feeling a bit hungry. It was at least an hour since breakfast.

Elmer read out to them what the book said:

"Sapphires. The Bight sapphires. Originally from Kashmir, these are thought to be the biggest and most valuable sapphires in the world. They have been in the possession of the Bight family since the thirteenth century. The present Duchess and Duke of Bight live modestly in a three-storey house on the Isle of Bight off the west coast of Britain. The sapphires, rumoured to be the size of cherries, have never been placed on public display despite many requests."

Platto and Hermione stared at each other miserably. Here they were with a real life solution to their pressing financial problems in the shape of a real American jeweller and they had no idea where the sapphires were or what had happened to them. In fact neither of

82

them had ever seen the sapphires and didn't know whether they were the size of golf balls or Maltesers. Until they had started to look for them, they had always assumed they were in the family safe in the cellar.

Elmer T. Pinewood Junior looked at their faces and sipped the tea which Beatrice had brought in. He helped himself to a fruit scone and spread it with raspberry jam and fresh cream.

"I understand," he said. "I understand. Don't say another word. Elmer T. Pinewood Junior may have worked mighty hard to get where he is today but he's not a hick. No sir. I quite understand. Family heirlooms must stay in the family."

The Duchess and Duke remained silent.

At last Hermione spoke.

"We don't know where they are," she said.

10

Comings and Goings

"So that's what happened to me and the dragon," said Seb when Floella had told him about the Healer and the message they had to give Jeremiah Gorse.

"Sapphires! That's what it's all about," said Floella. "Miss Squidger wanted the dragon so she could find out where these sapphires are and then steal them, I suppose. They must belong to the Duchess."

"Yes," said Seb. "Perhaps the dragon will tell us more about it when he wakes up. You know we'll have to stay here all night now, Floella, because he's not due to wake up for another twelve hours."

"Oh no," cried Floella. "I expect Baz and

Gaz have already got back to the Isle of Bight and told Miss Squidger. She'll get her hands on the sapphires before the Duchess even knows what's happening."

"No, don't be soft," said Seb. "She'll only know they're in Great Bootington and not on the island. She doesn't know exactly where they are."

"It's funny," said Floella. "The Healer told me we could stay with him, almost as if he knew. Perhaps he does know something about all this, because he's been to Great Bootington *and* he spent some of his childhood on the Isle of Bight. Perhaps the dragon came here on purpose."

"Never," said Seb. "He just couldn't fly any further. What could that old chap have to do with it?"

"It's a good thing the dragon's asleep anyway," said Floella. "We can put the medicine on and then come back in the morning and fly home. I'll get this beastly spear thing out first."

It was an awkward job smearing the sticky pale green mixture from the bottle all over the wing and they weren't sure whether they should remove the wire, wood and polyfilla first but decided against it.

"The dragon cream has to be dabbed – just a tiny spot the Healer said – on the worst parts every day till there's none left," said Floella. They worked their way carefully over the damaged wing.

"He'll probably wake up in a minute and ask for a drink of water," said Seb.

"I wish he would," said Floella. "I hope he's going to be all right. He must have been in dreadful pain. I don't like to leave him on his own."

"He'll be all right," said Seb. "I don't want to sleep on these marshes and I'm absolutely starving."

As they set off for the Healer's cottage, they discussed what they would tell their parents when they got back home again.

"It's all right for me really," said Seb. "I often spend two or three days in the holidays with my Dad so my Mum will probably think I'm at his house."

"I suppose I could say I was at my Auntie's,"

said Floella.

They woke up early in the morning and after a quick cup of coffee, they said good-bye to the Healer and Spadger and went to find the dragon. To their relief, the dragon was just stirring as they arrived. He felt very refreshed but had no memory at all of recent events. Floella and Seb told him all that had happened.

"Of course," said the dragon. "The sapphires. As long as the Duchess has the sapphires, she can always find the money to renew the lease. Otherwise the island goes up for sale. Alas that I should be cheated into helping that evil magician. How fortunate that you overheard it all, Seb. I must warn the Duchess at once."

Floella and Seb climbed on his back, he circled a few times round the bleak marshes of Upper Goolash and in no time at all they were on course for Great Bootington. The dragon dropped them off in a field and took off again for the Isle of Bight. (The Town Hall roof now had a temporary marquee erected on it to discourage its use as a dragonport.)

"Don't worry," said Floella. "She doesn't know exactly where the sapphires are. We shall just have to find them before she does."

"But they've had half a day's start," said the dragon as he flapped his wings. They'd sellotaped the tube of cream onto the side of his neck.

"See you Humzo," they called as he took off.

On the Isle of Bight the Duchess was sitting beneath the Moonberry Tree as she always did when she had a problem. The tree was huge and could have sheltered the occupants of an entire double-decker bus. As she sat on the grass, listening to the falleybirds singing their strange song, "Tu-fall-tu-whoo, tu-whoo-tu-fall" as they waved their scarlet fan-shaped tails, she absentmindedly felt for something to eat in her tapestry shoulder-bag. Her hand scrabbled about the bag in vain. She couldn't find an apple or banana, not even a piece of nougat or a chocolate marshmallow, her favourite. All she could find was her Japanese paper wallet. She looked into its inner pocket and took out a photograph. How long had that been there

she wondered? She must have found it somewhere in the house and popped it in her wallet
out of harm's way. It was an old photograph
of her great-grandmother who had been the
twenty-first Duchess. Hermione remembered
now that there had been some scandal about
her and she was hardly mentioned in the
family. She had run off and left her husband and child, her own grandmother who
had been the twenty-second Duchess. (Un-
like aristocratic families in the rest of Britain,
the line descended on the female side in the
Bight family from eldest daughter to eldest

daughter.) Nothing had ever happened like it in the family before or, if it had, it had all been hushed up.

The Duchess wondered about her great-grandmother. Where had she gone to? Had she ever wanted to return to the Island? According to what she had heard from her own mother, the twenty-third Duchess, she had died not long after leaving the island and had been buried 'abroad' which is how Isle of Bighters referred to the rest of the British Isles.

Now where was it she went, wondered the Duchess. Somewhere to do with hands was it? Or was it feet? She was interrupted in her thoughts by a whooshing noise. Looking up she was startled to see what could only be the Humzoala Dragon coming in to land on the Eastern Plains stretching below her. He had never been known to leave the island yet here he was returning from the direction of the May Strait. Something very strange was going on. She hurried down to meet him.

The dragon was pleased to find the Duchess waiting for him as soon as he landed and immediately began to tell her the whole story of what had been happening.

"Of course," she cried as he described his first landing-place. "Feet. *Boots*. Great Bootington. That's where my great-grandmother went."

The dragon, interrupted at what he felt to be a critical stage of the narrative, lapsed into an offended silence, until the Duchess hastened to tell him how much she admired his forethought and bravery and how grateful she was to him.

"You shall be suitably rewarded," she said, "for your outstandingly brave deeds. I shall recommend you for the I.B.C." (Isle of Bight Cross). The Humzoala dragon didn't seem very impressed with this.

"The only reward I could wish for ma'am," he said, "I regret is not in your gift."

"And what's that?" asked the Duchess in surprise.

"An heir," said the dragon mournfully. "I am the last of my line" and he went on to tell the rest of the story.

A family council was held back in the Bight

household, to which Mr Pinewood, as an interested party, had been invited.

"As I see it Duchess, if I can put a word in"
(everyone nodded, even Antonio) "this Miss
Squidger already knows about the sapphires
and is probably on her way, or already in,
Great Tootington – "

"Bootington," said Tamara.

"Ssh," said the Duke.

"So it is vital we leave immediately. Since
you say your great-grandmother died there, it
would be a good idea to try and remember
everything you can about her."

"We're trying to," said the Duchess and
Duke together, for Platto was writing a history
of the Bight family.

"But what about us?" cried Viola, Rosalind,
Perdita, Olivia, Tamara, Romeo, Hamlet and
Touchstone. (Antonio was busy chewing Flat
Harry's leg again.)

"How can we get there?" asked the Duchess. "Bight Airlines only runs Mondays and
Saturdays and there isn't a ferry till tomorrow
afternoon."

"No problem," said Elmer. "We'll all go.

How d'you think I got here? Not on Concorde. No sir. In my own private jet – it can seat up to thirty comfortably and it has a special service area for pets."

"Wicked."

"Shylock and Bottom are coming."

"A real plane?"

"Can I sit at the front?"

"Can I sit at the back?"

"I want to sit by the window."

"Do I *have* to come?"

The pandemonium which ensued was only brought to an end by Elmer standing up and saying, "I'll be leaving from the Eastern Plains in five minutes, Duchess." He winked at the Duke. "I'll see you there."

Beatrice rushed among them, stuffing feet into the tough boots all the Bight children wore, wiping dirty faces, doing up buttons, cramming all sorts of oddments into cupboards and vases, thrusting Bottom into a straw basket and putting a collar and lead on Shylock. The Duchess put on a clean turban and Platto took off his apron and picked up his straw hat. They were ready. Perdita slipped on a soggy

fishfinger which Bottom had abandoned at the foot of the stairs but was comforted by the promise of a seat by the window. Soon they were all comfortably disposed in the plane which had soft purple reclining seats. Under Elmer's instructions the Duke put on a cartoon video to keep the children amused.

"We'll be there in about forty minutes," Elmer said. "Fasten your seatbelts folks."

11

Jeremiah Gorse

Elmer was wrong however to think Miss Squidger had already started out for Great Bootington. Baz and Gaz had accidentally let slip what Grubb had told them about two children being on the dragon when it had left the Town Hall. Miss Squidger, fuming at their incompetence in not tracking them down, was undecided what to do.

"You snivelling dunderheads," she snarled. "They may have overheard everything. Then they too will know where the sapphires are."

She made sure, by means of Pogglow, that Baz and Gaz were telling the truth about the dragon's reply to the question and that they had not seen either of the children. Then she sent them away and spent the whole of Wednesday evening deciding what to do and finding out all she could about Great Booington and its inhabitants.

"I don't trust them," she said to Pogglow the next morning. "They're too stupid to find the sapphires on their own, but on the other hand, if they did find them, they might just keep them and not return at all. We're all going."

"Me too?" asked Pogglow in surprise. Miss Squidger always discouraged him from going out much on his own. She was afraid of someone else discovering his secret.

"Certainly," said Miss Squidger. "I shall need you. Go and pack a case."

"For how long?" asked Pogglow nervously.

"Who knows? But be certain of this. I shall not return without the sapphires."

They left in the helicopter for Great Booington, not all that long before the Duchess and family took off in Elmer's plane. Miss Squidger's crystal ball, wrapped in a seersucker tablecloth, was in Pogglow's suitcase. After Baz and Gaz had parked the helicopter on a patch of wasteland behind a church, Miss Squidger booked all four of them into the Flounder and Firkin in the High Street. A Union Jack flew from the roof and portraits of the Queen and Prince Philip adorned the walls. Miss Squidger booked two rooms, one large one with an adjoining bathroom and one small one. The large room was for her and the small one for Baz and Gaz and Pogglow. While these three were unpacking their bags and arguing over who should have which bed, Miss Squidger had removed the seersucker table-cloth and its contents. She drew the curtains of her room, locked the door and set her crys-tal ball down on the bedside table. Perhaps she could find out more about the sapphires if she knew what the Duchess was doing . . . or those children. She ripped a pillowcase off one of the pillows and rubbed the crystal ball with it. It became smoky. Shapes whirled. It cleared and she could make out the Duchess. She was . . .

Brrrrr Brrrrrrr Brrrrrrrrr Brrrrrrrrrrr.

Miss Squidger picked up the telephone in a rage as she saw the picture fade from the crystal and it became cloudy again. One second's lack of concentration and it was gone.

"Yes," she roared into the telephone.

"Welcome to the Flounder and Firkin," trilled a syrupy voice. "We would like to remind all our guests that we shall be having a Happy Hour in the lounge bar at 7PM. All drinks at half price. Should you wish for cocktails to be – "

Miss Squidger banged down the receiver without listening to any more and vented her anger by kicking the dressing-table. This was unwise as the front of the top drawer promptly fell off with a crash.

Thumping outside caused her to throw the tablecloth quickly over the crystal. Unlocking the door, she found a chambermaid with a tray of tea.

"Welcome to the Flounder and Firkin," said the maid, pushing past Miss Squidger and going over to place the tray on the bedside-table. Miss Squidger headed her off. "Pogglow," she roared while the maid looked from her to the dressing-table, the pillowslip and the table-cloth with a puzzled expression. As

Pogglow, dressed in an orange lurex shirt and matching velvet knickerbockers appeared, her expression changed to one of fright. She practically threw the tray at Pogglow as he advanced to take it and hurried out, bumping into Baz and Gaz in the passageway.

Pogglow wobbled but held gamely onto the tray.

"Er . . . where?"

"Take it away," screamed Miss Squidger. "Go back to your room the three of you and drink it. Go away."

Pogglow slunk off. Miss Squidger, giving up all hope of learning anything significant until after lunch, lay down and had a short nap. While she was sleeping, Floella was leafing through the telephone directory in Great Bootington Library. (She'd managed to convince her Dad that she'd stayed the night at her Aunt's and that she'd told him about it ages ago but he'd forgotten.) Seb was stroking a white mouse he had just bought at the pet shop. She'd found eight people called Gorse in it but only one of them had the initial J. Floella rang this one up but no one called Jeremiah lived there. She and Seb were arguing about ringing up the other seven people.

"We've got to," said Floella. "I promised him I'd do it as soon as possible. Then we can start thinking about the sapphires. We can take it in turns to ring. Do put that thing away. It gives me the creeps."

While they were looking for sufficient change for a possible seven calls, the Duchess and her family landed on a large field on the outskirts of town. They made their way towards the nearest building, a five-storey one with some newer smaller buildings a short distance away.

"Let's go in there," suggested the Duchess, "and find out where there's a good hotel." The children bounded on ahead except for Antonio who sat in his push-chair, clasping Flat Harry while Beatrice pushed him. Elmer, the Duke, carrying Bottom in the basket, and the Duchess, with Shylock tucked under one arm, strolled behind.

Strangely enough, no one seemed to be about. They walked into the large building through a back entrance and made their way

up some stairs. The lift was too small to take all of them.

"It's a hospital," said Elmer looking at the board by the lift. "I suggest we go to the third floor. There's a lounge and vending machines."

"Good idea," said the Duchess cheerfully.

While the children, supplied with ample ten, twenty and five pence pieces occupied themselves at the vending machines, the Duchess and Duke and Elmer sat down to discuss their plans over plastic cups of coffee. Several people in dressing-gowns were also in the lounge, dozing or watching television. A very old man sat in a wheelchair near the window. Near him was a youngish pregnant woman reading a book. This was Floella's Mum. The Duchess rewound her turban as she listened to the Duke and Elmer talking about the twenty-first Duchess.

"At last," sighed Floella. "Someone's answering."

"Hello? Margaret Gorse speaking."

"Er . . . Is Mr Gorse in?" asked Floella.

They were down to the last Gorse on the list.

"My husband's at the Town Hall," said a stiff voice. "Is it something important?"

"Would that be Mr Jeremiah Gorse?"

"Oh I see. My father-in-law has been in Great Bootington Hospital for the last six weeks. I took it you were referring to my husband, Mr Malachi Gorse, the Chief Executive officer. If – "

"Thank you very much," interrupted Floella. "Goodbye."

"He must be very old," said Seb. "Come on then. The sooner we deliver that letter, the sooner we can start looking for the sapphires. Come on Soppitoe." (This was the mouse).

"I can see Mum too," said Floella. "But I don't know how on earth we'll find the sapphires. They could be anywhere."

Like the Bight family, they entered the hospital by the back entrance and made their way up to the third floor.

"There's Mum," said Floella. "I thought she'd be in here. She hates staying in bed. Come on Seb."

"It's full of children," said Seb as they

went in, "and there's a dog."

Bottom, sniffing the presence of an alien from within the cat-basket, began to miaow. Seb pushed Soppitoe to the bottom of his pocket.

"Mum," said Floella after she'd hugged her and introduced Seb, "we're looking for someone called Jeremiah Gorse. He's in the hospital somewhere and I've got a letter for him."

The old man in the chair looked up. "I'm Jeremiah Gorse," he said. "I wasn't expecting a letter."

Floella and Seb sat down beside him while he eagerly tore open the envelope.

"Graciousome Graciousomy," he said. (Just like the Healer thought Floella.) "To think of my old friend Theo Squidger still being alive."

There was a moment's shocked silence.

"Did you say . . . Squidger?" asked Floella.

"Yes. That's right."

"Is he that Miss Squidger's brother?" Seb asked Floella while the old man was reading his letter.

"He said he had a sister but they'd quarrelled. It's O.K., Seb. He's not like her. Look how he healed the dragon."

"Are you sure?" Seb said doubtfully. "This might be a trick."

"So how is my old friend?" asked Jeremiah in a light crackly voice like a piece of paper being torn.

"Quite well," said Floella, "but . . ."

The old man wasn't listening however. He was feeling in his dressing-gown pockets. "I'm going to give you something for bringing me this message."

"It doesn't matter," said Floella, as he rummaged in a carrier-bag near his feet. "The Healer mended the Dragon's wing so that was the least I could do in return."

As she said this the room went suddenly quiet and Floella looked round to see not only her mother but also Elmer, the Duchess and the Duke all staring at her.

"Did you say 'dragon' dear?" her mother said in a loud voice. "Was that the dragon on the Town Hall roof?"

Floella could tell that the others, although they were not still looking her way, were listening to this. Fortunately, Jeremiah Gorse found what he was looking for. He looked round him furtively before giving her a rather dirty bag. "There you are little lady," he said, patting Floella's hand with his own dry papery one, "marbles. All littl'uns like marbles. I've had these for years. I always carry them about with me." He winked at her and coughed with the effort of saying so much.

Floella thanked him. She didn't really like marbles much but it was kind of him to give her something he'd been carrying around with him for so long. Seb had lost interest and was reading a geographical magazine he'd found on a table. It had a really good article about polar bears in it.

At that moment two excited nurses appeared and began hustling all the patients back into their wards. They looked very put out to see all the visitors.

"Must be official invites," said one nurse. "No one else is allowed in till afterwards."

The other nurse rolled her eyes when she noticed the cat-basket and Shylock.

" 'Bye little miss," said Jeremiah as he was

wheeled off, protesting, to his ward.

"You're lucky being here now," her mother said as she walked back to her ward which was just next door. "I thought they weren't letting anyone in."

"Why not?" asked Floella.

"The visit," her mother said impatiently. "Why d'you think I've had my hair done? Mind you, your Dad could have done it much better."

"Jeepers O'Riley," said Seb who had put down the article on polar bears in disgust, finding a large piece had been torn off. "We shouldn't be here at all. D'you realise the Queen's coming? What shall we do?"

"I'd forgotten all about it," said Floella. "We'll just have to stay here now till it's all over. We can't go dashing about. Listen."

A fanfare and a distant outburst of cheering told them the Queen had already arrived.

12

Miss Squidger Locates the Sapphires

After a meal of blood pudding and stewed prunes, Miss Squidger felt much revived. She rubbed up the crystal ball once more. Blurred shapes began to appear.

"Aha. The Duchess has left the Isle of Bight," she said. "Let's see if I can find out more about those children."

The next picture she saw in the crystal was a small black girl in jeans, T-shirt and trainers talking to a small white boy also dressed in jeans, T-shirt and trainers. Miss Squidger clasped her hands together in triumph.

"Those must be the two children Grubb saw. We're getting closer. I feel it. *Now* to find where the sapphires are."

She gazed fixedly at the crystal ball and clenched her fists. A faint picture appeared . . .

"Yes," said Miss Squidger. "It's a HOSPITAL."

She collected Baz and Gaz from the lounge where they were playing Snakes and Ladders in a corner and sharing a small can of Pepsi-Cola, which was all Miss Squidger would allow them.

"Come," she said. "We're going to collect the sapphires." She snapped her fingers and they all jumped to their feet and followed her immediately. "Success at last, Pogglow," she said.

Pogglow, who had been enjoying a freer life than he had been accustomed to on the Isle of Bight, tried to look suitably pleased, but all he got for his pains was, "And take that silly look off your face. Here, carry this" and the crystal ball, re-wrapped in the tablecloth and placed in a canvas bag, was thrust into his hands.

"Now," said Miss Squidger, "this definitely calls for some shape-changing. Unfortunately, we're on the mainland, where my magic is not

so strong but these shapes should last long
enough for our needs."

She made a few passes in the air. Baz
and Gaz and Pogglow vanished. In their place
stood three nurses, two lanky ones and a third,
squat one. Miss Squidger was annoyed. She
had expected them to be all the same size in
their false shapes. She spoke some words and
made more signs and was transformed into a
man in a white coat with a stethoscope slung
round his neck.

"Come along nurses. No one will stop us
now."

Seb and Floella sat together in the hospital lounge near the window, while Elmer, the Duchess and the Duke sat on a brown corduroy sofa at the opposite end. The children were all sitting quietly watching the film of "The Wizard of Oz" which they had seen several times before. They were all eating crisps, chocolate and biscuits and sipping various fruit juices.

"It's a bit awkward," the Duchess was saying to Elmer, "isn't it Platto? We've not really had much to do with the mainland branch of the Royal Family since that affair in the eighteenth century. I would never have come in here, had I known she was paying a visit. It's most embarrassing."

Elmer didn't see what all the fuss was about. "Those children over there," he said to Platto, "they must be the ones who helped the dragon, from what they were saying earlier."

"Really?" said Platto as he wrote in another solution to his crossword. "I think we ought to thank them. If it wasn't for them, we should never have known the sapphires were in Great Bootington."

Elmer went over and started talking to Floella and Seb. They were a bit suspicious at first but when he took them over to the Duchess and told them all about the Dragon's safe return to the island, they were delighted. The Duchess hugged both of them, the Duke shook them each by the hand and Elmer patted them on the back. Then they were introduced to Beatrice who presented each of the children to them in turn. Last of all was Antonio who insisted on Flat Harry being introduced as well. Then it was Bottom and Shylock's turn. Shylock settled himself on Seb's lap.

"And this is Soppitoe," said Seb, holding him well out of reach of curious hands and paws.

Soon all the children were on the carpet together having a game of tiddlywinks. The Duchess put Soppitoe into her turban for safety. A sudden loud burst of clapping told them that the Queen was now in the adjoining ward. She must have come in at the other end of the building. At the same time, the lift on the other side hummed to a stop and out strode a doctor followed by three nurses. As soon as the doctor saw the Bight family, he muttered angrily to the nurses. Then he saw Seb and Floella.

"Those are the ones," he hissed. Two tall nurses advanced and caught hold of them.

"Let go," screamed Floella dropping the bag old Mr Gorse had given her as one of the nurses twisted her arm. Seb kicked one of them as she and a short fat nurse tried to stuff him into a sack.

"Help! Help!"

"Hey, what's going on?" demanded Elmer T. Pinewood Junior dashing forward. "Leave those kids alone."

"They've escaped from a children's home," said the doctor curtly. "They are extremely dangerous. Mentally disturbed you understand."

"Pifflebosh," said the Duchess, rising to her feet. She took off her turban and laid into the short fat nurse with it. "Put them down. At once." Soppitoe leapt out of the turban and bit the nurse on the nose.

Shylock, eager to join the fray, snapped at the first thing he could lay teeth on which turned out to be one of the tall nurses' left hand. Not to be outdone, Bottom scratched the doctor, alias Miss Squidger, on the face. Gaz attacked the Duchess with a couple of cushions and an umbrella. The Duke, outraged, swiped at him with a rolled-up newspaper and a brief-case while Elmer tripped up Pogglow. The children, seeing their parents and newly-found friends being attacked, threw themselves into the fight with gusto. Though small, they had lots of energy, sharp teeth and nails and tough boots.

The crystal ball, unheeded, rolled out of the canvas bag, unwound itself from the tablecloth and rolled across the floor in full view of any-one not too occupied in fighting to see it. Miss Squidger, who had three children attached to one leg, tried in vain to grab it. The Duchess, sitting firmly on top of Pogglow saw it roll past her.

"These aren't real nurses or a real doctor," she cried. "Look there. That's a crystal ball. There's WITCHERY going on."

She snatched it up and crashed it as hard as she could against the wall. It smashed

into thousands of brightly-coloured shards
which glittered for a few seconds and then
turned black. At this moment the doors
from the adjoining ward opened and Her
Majesty, accompanied by the Matron, Arthur
Greenhalgh and various other dignitaries of
Great Bootington, advanced into the lounge
and came to a sudden, shocked halt.

13

The Sapphires Restored

"You never saw anything like it," Arthur Greenhalgh said afterwards to his wife. "Utter blinking chaos. There was this woman as big as a bus sat on a short fat nurse, chairs all over the place, a man wearing a straw hat astride a doctor trying to tie his legs together with a stethoscope. Tables and books and vases of flowers overturned. Bits of black glass all over the floor. And children. The place was swarming with them. Five of them were sitting on two more nurses, there was a dog barking its head off, a cat sitting on top of a television set which was upside-down but still going (the telly I mean) and, blow me, if there wasn't a blithering white mouse running about among a lot of what looked like marbles. You never heard such a din. And the language the nurses and doctor were using you just wouldn't credit coming from the caring professions. Oh, shocking it was."

"After all the preparations," sympathized Mavis. "What a shame. Whatever did the Queen make of it all?"

"Eh, she's a marvel," said Arthur. "A ruddy marvel. Complete pokerface. We just turned round and marched straight back out again. The Matron took her down the other way and I got on the blower to the police. Then I went back sharpish to help those nurses and the doctor. But by heck, by the time I got back there the police were already there. Of course the grounds were crawling with them 'cause they'd found this aeroplane. Anyway," said Arthur, "what I don't understand is, by the time I'd got back the police had arrested two blokes in red boiler-suits, a short fat freaky-looking chap in an orange velvet knickerbocker suit, would you believe, and a tall thin right nasty-looking old woman."

"You what?" said Mavis. "I don't understand. You didn't mention them before."

"No," said Arthur, "on account of they weren't there before."

"And what about the nurses and doctor?" asked Mavis.

"That's the funny thing," said Arthur. "They weren't anywhere to be seen. And it seemed this enormous woman as big as a bus and a right good-looker too, turned out to be a Duchess and most of the children were hers. It seems these other people came in and started attacking them."

"Ee, Arthur, I'm sure you've got it all muddled," said Mavis. "Probably too busy looking at this Duchess. It doesn't sound right to me. Poor Queen. What must she have thought?"

"Anyway," said Arthur. "That wasn't the end of it. There was this American crawling about on the floor picking up marbles. Jeremiah Gorse had given them to one of these kids, not one of the Duchess'. Her mother's in the hospital having a baby."

"Whose mother?" asked Mavis. "The Duchess?"

"No, Mavis, don't be daft. This girl. Floella

she's called. This Jeremiah Gorse is a very old chap. He's the father of Malachi down at the Town Hall."

"I know," said Mavis. "About a hundred and fifty at a rough guess."

"It seems Floella brought him a letter from an old friend he hadn't seen for years. From Upper Goolash. This chap told him to give her these marbles, only they weren't really marbles. He'd had them for years. Evidently there was some secret attached to them because Malachi said they weren't rightly his at all."

"What a tale," said Mavis. "What with dragons and fights with disappearing nurses and enormous Duchesses, I'll bet you're going to say that it all had something to do with the marbles that weren't really marbles."

"Are you right or are you right?" said Arthur. "Turns out this American chappie creeping around the floor was a jeweller. Half of them weren't marbles at all. They were sapphires."

"What?" said Mavis. "Go on Arthur! You're making it all up."

"No," said Arthur. "It's one hundred per

cent true. Anyway, it turns out Floella and her friend Seb and Soppitoe – "

"Who's Soppitoe?" sighed Mavis.

"That was the name of his mouse," said Arthur. "These two kids, the American and the Duchess and her family had all been looking for the sapphires, and the others – the ones they arrested – had been trying to steal them. This old friend of Jeremiah's had warned him in the letter not to tell the girl they were sapphires of course, unless he was alone with her, on account of all these dodgy characters."

"But what were they doing in Great Bootington Hospital?" persisted Mavis, "and how did they know the jewels were there?"

"It's all to do with Jeremiah. Evidently the Duchess' great grandmother ran off with him taking these sapphires with her."

"What? That desiccated old haddock?" said Mavis.

"Now be fair Mavis. Jeremiah's well past his prime. We all know that. But the girls really fancied him when he was a lad, so they say."

"But Arthur, I still don't understand. What

did the dragon have to do with it?"

Arthur shook his head. "Nay, don't ask me. It's been a right odd week. I'll never forget opening them doors and seeing everyone in a heap on the floor clobbering one another. Never."

14

The End

As expected, Elmer T. Pinewood Junior
bought the sapphires from the Duchess, all
except one which was kept to be handed down
to Rosalind as the eldest daughter and a future
Duchess. The Duchess was able to renew the
lease of the island for another nine hundred
and ninety nine years and since Miss Squidger
never returned, she was able to release Sparrow, Scum her dog, and various other people
and animals who had been imprisoned in her
service. In addition they were able to build a
much larger house sufficient for all their large
family and the additional helpers they were
now able to pay for.

Floella and Seb were frequent visitors to

the island and were often to be found either at the Duchess' house or out on the Blue Hill with the Humzoala dragon who was awarded the Isle of Bight Cross in a special ceremony beneath the Moonberry Tree. After some years the dragon began to peak and pine and the Duchess was obliged to send someone on a special quest to find him a mate. Baz and Gaz and Pogglow spent a short time in prison and then returned to the island where they appeared to settle down quite happily away from the baleful influence of Miss Squidger. Grubb, however, did not reappear either on the island or in Great Bootington after his release.

Elmer returned to Florence, Oregon, the United States of A, the proud possessor of the Bight sapphires. He issued invitations to all of them to visit him whenever they wished. They all went to see him off at Bootrow Airport where the Duchess pressed a carrier-bagful of home-made scones upon him and the Duke gave him a book of crossword puzzles. All the Bight children plus Flat Harry, Bottom and Shylock clustered round for a kiss and

a cuddle while Seb and Floella promised to write.

What of Miss Squidger? She managed, without the help of her crystal ball, to remove herself from prison and was never seen again

in that part of the world. Nor did she ever
return to Upper Goolash to disturb the peace
of her brother, the Healer. Whether her path
ever crossed those of Floella, Seb, the Bight
family or the Humzoala dragon again is a different matter and another story.